One Night
in the Zoo

For Ian Craig, who made this book possible,
with love and thanks

First American Edition 2010
Kane Miller, A Division of EDC Publishing

Originally published in England by HarperCollins Publishers Ltd under the title:
ONE NIGHT IN THE ZOO
Text and illustrations copyright © Kerr-Kneale Production Ltd. 2009

For information contact:
Kane Miller, A Division of EDC Publishing
P.O. Box 470663
Tulsa, OK 74147-0663
www.kanemiller.com
www.edcpub.com

Library of Congress Control Number: 2009907132

Printed and bound in China

1 2 3 4 5 6 7 8 9 10
ISBN: 978-1-935279-37-2

One Night in the Zoo

Judith Kerr

Kane Miller
A DIVISION OF EDC PUBLISHING

One magical, moonlit night in the zoo

An elephant jumped in the air and flew.
But nobody knew.

Then a crocodile and a kangaroo
Set off on a bicycle made for two,

And three lions did tricks which astonished a gnu.
But nobody knew.

Four bears cooked a squid and squidgeberry stew

Which turned five flamingos
from pink to blue.

Six rabbits climbed a giraffe for the view.
But nobody knew.

Seven tigers sneezed: Atchoo! Atchoo!
Atchoo! Atchoo! Atchoo! Atchoo!
ATCHOO! And their seven sneezes blew
The feathers off a cockatoo.

Eight monkeys stuck them back with glue.
But nobody knew.

Then in the sky a pinkish hue
Broke through the dark, and as it grew
Nine owls cried, "Woo! Terwitterwoo!
The night is fading! Quickly! Shoo!
Back in your cages, all of you!"

The sun got up. The keeper, too.
Ten cocks crowed, "Cockadoodledoo!
He's coming! Quick! He's almost due!"

The keeper and his trusty crew
Found all the animals back on view
(excepting only one or two).

"They look so tired," he said. "All through
That moonlit night what *did* they do?"
But nobody knew…

…Except you!

And here they are again.

3

5

6

8

10

GR

10-16